CH

For my sweet sisters—
Sandra Fergins, who hardly talks at all,
and Marcia Shelf, who fills in the silences.
Love, A.S.M.

To Pamela
S.V.

THIS STORY IS BASED ON A TALE
FROM ACCRA IN GHANA, WEST AFRICA.

Text copyright © 1995 by Angela Shelf Medearis
Illustrations copyright © 1995 by Stefano Vitale

Library of Congress Cataloging-in-Publication Data

Medearis, Angela Shelf, 1956 –
Too much talk / Angela Shelf Medearis ;
illustrated by Stefano Vitale.—1st ed.
Summary: A retelling of a traditional West African tale about a
king who refuses to believe that yams, fish, and cloth can talk
until his throne agrees with him.
ISBN 1-56402-323-0
[1. Folklore—Africa, West.] I. Vitale, Stefano, ill. II.Title.
PZ8.1.M468To   1995
398.2'0966'02—dc20 [E]   95-16184

2 4 6 8 10 9 7 5 3 1

Printed in Hong Kong

This book was typeset in Maiandra.
The pictures in this book were done in oil paints on wood.

Candlewick Press
2067 Massachusetts Avenue
Cambridge, Massachusetts 02140

TOO
MUCH TALK

Angela Shelf Medearis

ILLUSTRATED BY
Stefano Vitale

CANDLEWICK PRESS
CAMBRIDGE, MASSACHUSETTS

One day a farmer in West Africa
went out to gather some yams.

While he was digging, a yam said to him,
"You did not water me. You did not weed
me. And here you come to dig me up!"
"Well!" said the farmer. First he looked
around. Then he looked at his dog and
said, "Were you talking to me?"

"No," barked the dog. "It was the yam."

"Aiyeee!" screamed the farmer. He ran and he ran, uphill and downhill. And he ran and he ran, downhill and uphill. He ran until he met a man who was carrying some fish.

"Why are you running in the heat of the day?" said the fisherman.

"Well," said the farmer, "first my yam talked and then my dog talked!"

"Oh," said the fisherman, "that can't happen."

"Oh, yes it can," the fish said to them. "Aiyeee!" screamed the farmer and the fisherman. They ran and they ran, uphill and downhill. And they ran and they ran, downhill and uphill. They ran until they met a man who was weaving some cloth.

"Why are you running in the heat of the day?" the weaver said.

"Well," said the farmer, "first my yam talked, then my dog talked, and then the fish talked."

"Oh," said the weaver, "that can't happen."

"Oh, yes it can," the cloth said to them. "Aiyeee!" screamed the farmer and the fisherman and the weaver. They ran and they ran, uphill and downhill. And they ran and they ran, downhill and uphill. They ran until they came to a woman who was swimming.

"Ahhhh," said the swimmer as she glided through the water. "Why are you running in the heat of the day?"

"Well," said the farmer, "first my yam talked, then my dog talked, then the fish talked, and then the cloth talked."

"Oh," said the swimmer as she did the backstroke, "that can't happen."

"Oh, yes it can," the water said to her. "Aiyeee!" screamed the farmer and the fisherman, the weaver and the swimmer. They ran and they ran, uphill and downhill. And they ran and they ran, downhill and uphill. They ran until they came to the house of the chief.

The chief came out and sat on his royal chair. He said to them, "Why are you running in the heat of the day?"

"Well," said the farmer, "first my yam talked, then my dog talked, then the fish talked, then the cloth talked, and then the water talked."

"Talk, talk, talk!" said the chief. "Too much talk! Yams don't talk! Fish don't talk! Cloth doesn't talk! And water doesn't talk! All this foolish talk will disturb the village! Go away, before I throw you in jail!"

So they all ran away.

"Imagine," said the chief, "a talking yam! How can that be?"

"So true," said the chair. "Whoever heard of a talking yam?"

"Aiyeee!" screamed the chief.
And he ran uphill and downhill and
was never seen again.